THE ADVENTURES OF
A WRITER-IN-TRAINING

JORIS CHAMBLAIN - AURÉLIE NEYRET

Cici's journal

THE ADVENTURES OF
A WRITER-IN-TRAINING

:01

First Second

New York

For Part One...

I thank my parents and my friends for their generous and motivating support.

Thank you to Joris for seeing the potential for Cici in my pencil and helping put so much love into it.
Thank you to Barbara and Clotilde for making this adventure possible and coming along with us during this long undertaking. And, finally, thank you to my Nico for his support every day and his help beyond worth.

Aurélie

Life is a road on which we hold each other's hand.
Huge thanks:
—to my parents and my sisters for having accompanied me on my first steps with love, without ever putting the least obstacle in the way of my dreams.
—to Christophe A., who, though he doesn't know it, showed me the way I wanted to take, and to Stéphane B. for having corrected my first steps on the walk, my new path.
—to Nicolas M. for showing me the secret to always walking right. I will never forget. And to Djilali D. for making sure I never stepped off the road. I know what's waiting for me if that happens!
—to Aurélie N., Barbara C., and Clotilde V. for crossing my path and joining me for this part of the journey, this lovely adventure. I hope we'll be together a long way!
—to you, dear reader, for pausing on your route to discover our side path.

—and, finally, thank you, Marjorie C., for joining my path and walking at my side, brightening our way onward.

Joris

For Part Two...

In memory of Aimé, my grandfather.
Thank you to my friends and family for their unstinting support.
Thanks also to Clotilde, Barbara, and Adeline for believing in us and for all their involvement.
Finally, special thanks to Nico, without whom this book would not be what it is, for many reasons.

Aurélie

I dedicate this book:
—to my grandparents, who Cici did not have the chance to know. I hope that wherever you are, they have good bookstores.

—to the little hidden message that slept for fifty years in a treasure chest, before a little boy could discover it...

Joris

Once upon a time...

When I was little, I promised myself that if I ever had a secret journal, it would start just like that.

I love to read stories, and my favorites all begin with "Once upon a time..."

So Once upon a time ... there was me, Cici!

That's me, Cici!

I'm ten and a half years old, and my dream is to become an author. I love to write. And I love to read novels, comics, and science magazines. My mother always tells me that a good vocabulary is the best weapon in life. I didn't used to understand why. Now I do. When you read you discover things and travel places, but you also learn the meanings of words and how to use them. It's very important to understand things, and to pay attention to what we say.

My trick for telling stories is to observe people, to imagine their lives, their secrets. We all have a secret inside us, something we never talk about. Something that makes us who we are.

So when I meet people I always try to dig out that "thing." I've been doing that since I was little. I don't even know why anymore. I think it helps me understand them better.

Right now, my friends and I are observing someone really <u>mysterious</u>.

I hope we finally figure out his secret.
Then I could tell his whole story.
I already have the first line!

It'll start like this:

« Once upon a time... »

Go, Detective Cici!!!

Once upon a time,
a little girl who was

Mom! ♡

MOM

Now that I've started my story, I should be a good author and introduce my characters.

And who else could I start with but this lady? My mom!

I live with her in a big house in the country that she inherited from her great uncle, or something like that, I'm not totally sure.

She bought me this journal. She told me: "If you want to be an author, you have to write! And a personal journal is a good start." That's my mom!

She doesn't love it that I hang out so much with Mrs. Flores, our neighbor. She wants me to play more with girls my own age. But she believes in my dream to be an author, and this journal is how she's helping me get there!

She isn't up to date on all my little investigations into people's lives. I don't think she'd be so happy about those. Of course, I've never asked her...

She doesn't always listen, but I love her anyway— she's my mom! One day I'll write a book just for her. In it, I'll finally tell her something important: thanks.

There are all sorts of little words like that. Words that aren't easy to say, that stay stuck at the bottom of my throat.

Does my mom have her own words that refuse to come out?

my friends!

↓ ↓

♡ Lena and Erica, ↘

my friends for life.

I always think of them as a pair.
They just belong together. Sometimes I get
a little jealous of how close they are...

We've all known each other since we were really little.
Well, since I moved to town. Lena and Erica have
known each other since they knew how to walk.

Lena is the sweetest ever. She has a sharp eye
and the soul of an artist. Someday she's going to be
a famous photographer. Plus she's going to be an
auntie soon, since her sister is expecting a baby.
Lena can't wait to take tons of pictures of that
baby! In the meantime, she's practicing on her
little brother!

I love how easygoing and open she is. She says what
she thinks, but she never makes fun of people. Sometimes
I wish I were a little more like her...

Erica is the complete opposite of Lena. She complains
constantly, but she has a good heart. She has four big
brothers, so she knows how to defend herself! I don't even
notice her complaining anymore, it's just
part of her. Respect and honesty
are important to her parents
and for their kids too. So Erica
hates it when things don't line up.
Complaining is how she questions
things, to try to shake things up,
to make them better. And I
respect her for that.

♡ Lena, ♡ ☆ Erica,

you're my
best friends!

I met Mrs. Flores for the first time at school. She was doing a reading. It's really cool, having a famous writer living in our own town. She did some writing exercises with us, and I had a lot of fun.

Annabelle Flores

After meeting her that day,
I knew that I wanted to write books too.

We became friends, and now I spend a lot of time with her, learning more about writing and asking lots of questions...even if my mom isn't always happy about that. Sometimes I have to visit her in secret!

But as I write this, I realize I really don't know a lot about her. Mrs. Flores lives in a huge mansion, all alone. Does she have a husband? Kids? I wouldn't dare ask her. I'm not sure how she'd react... She keeps her distance, and she doesn't get a lot of visitors. But she doesn't seem unhappy about it.

On the other hand, she knows a lot of things about me. I think she can read me like an open book! Sometimes it's embarrassing that I can't hide anything from her! Even when I don't say a thing, she understands what I'm feeling.
        I wish I could do that. Maybe you get that power when you grow up ...

Someday when I'm big ...→   Ms. Cici,
super-amazing writ-

Erica wants pink curtains in the hideout, Lena wants plaid, and I want little birds.

Arrgh, it's never finished!

our super hideout!

Before a writer starts the plot, you have to set the scene.

My friends and I have a great spot for adventures:

our secret hideout!

Erica's brothers helped us build it, and they found some old furniture in the trash.

It's kind of goofy.

We just can't agree on the curtains.

But I'm sure we'll figure it out.

We were up in the hideout when we discovered

Mr. Mysterious for the first time.

I have to tell you about this guy!

door

windows

table

TRUNK

couch

recycled planks from L___
paint
nails
saw (with Erica's da___

Here's how it all started...

Lena's the one who saw him for the first time. We were playing in our secret hideout. Erica was probably complaining about something: the wind coming in through the boards, or how uncomfortable the couch was... and I was writing down decoration ideas for the hideout...

Lena was taking pictures of the birds, and then suddenly she froze. She noticed something in the background. An old man was coming out of the woods, completely covered with paint in every color. It was spooky! He had it on his hands, his shoes, even his face.

He wandered away and disappeared. All three of us were a little scared, even if Erica said she wasn't. We all hurried home, and we swore we wouldn't set foot in the woods again anytime soon.

Think, Cici!

But once I was safe at home, I started to ask myself some questions. Who was he? Why all those colors? I spent the whole night imagining lots of things about his life. I wanted to get to the bottom of it. So the next day, I went to the hideout by myself and waited. But I didn't see him again. I went back every day, hoping to spot him. It must have taken a week before I saw him come out of the forest again. It was the same thing: clothes covered with paint, and disappearing on the path. I didn't dare go after him.

Ever since I saw him go poof like that, I've had only one goal: to be right there the moment he ducks into the trees! Then, maybe, I'll be able to crack this mystery...?

Mr. Mysterious

Today is Sunday, and the church bells are ringing at 9 a.m.

Dong, Dong, Dong

the hideout

DONG DONG DONG DONG DONG

CICI?!?

WHAT ARE YOU DOING UP SO EARLY? AND ON A SUNDAY TOO?

WE FINISHED BUILDING OUR HIDEOUT IN THE WOODS. WE'RE SUPPOSED TO MEET UP EARLY TO DECORATE IT.

A HIDEOUT, HUH? BACK IN MY DAY WE CALLED THAT "SNEAKING OFF WITH A SWEETHEART"!

SHEESH!

JUST DON'T STAY OUT TOO LATE, ALL RIGHT?

DON'T WORRY, MOM! I'VE GOT MY CELL PHONE, JUST IN CASE! SEE YOU LATER!

THAT WAS MOM'S GREAT IDEA:
A "JUST IN CASE" CELL PHONE.
THAT'S HOW SHE PUTS IT.
WHO'S IT REALLY FOR, HER OR
ME? MOM IS SOMETHING ELSE.
I'M GOING TO WRITE A BOOK
ABOUT HER ONE DAY,
FOR SURE.

WRITING BOOKS,
IMAGINING PEOPLE'S
LIVES...

...BRINGING
THEM TO
LIFE THROUGH
ADVENTURES,
IMAGINING THE
DANGERS THEY'LL
FACE...

...WHO
THEY'LL HATE,
WHO THEY'LL
LOVE...

LIKE RAMON
OVER THERE! DID
HE FINALLY DECIDE
TO GIVE JULIE
FLOWERS?

ULYSSES IS
SUCH A ROMANTIC.
HE LOVES LOVE
STORIES.

IT'S LIKE
ULYSSES KEEPS
THAT STORE
OPEN JUST FOR
HIM!

OR GUY, AT
THE FARMER'S
MARKET.

HE SAYS
HE LOST HIS LEG
UNDER A TRACTOR,
BUT I'M SURE
THAT'S NOT WHAT
HAPPENED!

Guy is
really a
pirate!

And a
killer shark
ate his
leg!

And these days
he digs in the
dirt so he can
find pirate
treasure!

9

COME ON, CICI. YOU CAN DO IT! WATCH CAREFULLY, AND FIGURE IT OUT!

A LITTLE LATER...

MR. MYSTERIOUS, RIGHT ON TIME.

HEY... WHAT'S THAT...?

WO-O-OW!

12

ARGH! EVERY TIME!

I LOOK AWAY FOR A SECOND, AND MR. MYSTERIOUS VANISHES!

HOW AM I SUPPOSED TO SPY ON HIM?

HE CAN'T HAVE GONE FAR...

HUH?! NO WAY HE COULD DISAPPEAR SO FAST!

WHA—?!

HI!

HEY!

I NEED TO TELL YOU ABOUT—

HI, GIRLS!

DID YOU ALL HAVE FUN AT THE TREE HOUSE THIS MORNING?

UH... YEAH. YEAH!

RIGHT, THE TREE HOUSE!

SEE YOU LATER, MOM.

BYE, MS. ARMAND!

THANKS FOR COVERING FOR ME BACK THERE. IT'S BETTER IF MY MOM THINKS I'M WITH YOU!

WE'RE USED TO IT.

OFF WE GO! TIME FOR HOURS OF SPYING! WHEE.

IT'S NOT MY FAULT HE'S SO INTERESTING!

ARE YOU GOING TO SPY ON YOUR MYSTERY GUY AGAIN?

17

18

MAYBE HE ATE IT?

UGH, GROSS!

DON'T BE SILLY.

WHAT? WE NEVER SAW THAT RACCOON AGAIN EITHER!

Maybe he rescues animals and then sets them free?

THEN WHAT ABOUT THE PAINT?

THIS IS A JOB FOR CHIEF DETECTIVE CICI!

YOU CAN COUNT ON ME TO SOLVE THIS MYSTERY!

HE'S ON THE MOVE! LET'S GO!

20

21

WHAT *IS* THIS THING??!

I'M NOT SO SURE I WANT TO FIND OUT!

AND WHAT'S ON THE OTHER SIDE?!

LET'S GET OUT OF HERE!

ERICA'S RIGHT!

OKAY... LET'S GO!

WHAT A DOWNPOUR! I'M SOAKED!

MY MOM'S GOING TO KILL ME!!!

ME TOO...

LET'S COME BACK SOON! I'M DESPERATE TO KNOW WHAT'S HIDING BEHIND THAT WALL!

YEAH, WE CAN TELL!

- cage?
- paint (all colors)
  ↳ a lot of colors for repainting a building... arrrggh!

me, losing my mind.

photo taken by Lena!

Mr. Mysterious!

The first time Lena saw him she took his picture by accident! And she never takes sneak photos! But she gave this one to me, which is good, because it's full of clues!

My friends and I have a lot of questions about Mr. Mysterious! We each have a different theory:

Erica's theory:

He eats the animals. He chooses a new one each week.

• Problem: What would he do if he wanted to eat a giraffe?

Lena's theory:

He frees the animals in the woods.

• Problem: Why carry a parrot the whole way and <u>then</u> open the cage?

• Problem #2: If he wanted to free a giraffe, how would he do it?

My theory:

He's painting a castle (or a haunted house!) from top to bottom.

• Problem: Why haven't we ever seen it in the woods?

...into the ...e animals

Cici Holmes?
Sherlock Cici?

To conduct a proper investigation, one must gather the facts (like Sherlock Holmes).

- Mr. Mysterious is only seen in the woods on the weekend.
- Gets there around 10 a.m., leaves around 7 p.m.
- We found a wall that cuts the woods in half... Is there a link to Mr. Mysterious?

wall!
what's behind it?

Next, one must conduct interviews. Back to town!

- The baker, like most of the people I interrogated, doesn't know what I'm talking about.
- The retired policeman says the photo is too blurry to figure out what he's doing.
- Ms. Galinier doesn't know and doesn't care who he is as long as he doesn't step on her mushrooms.
- Guy the pirate farmer has never seen this sailor on board his ship.
- I didn't interrogate Mom. If I tried, she'd find out about my investigation, and she'd definitely stop me from spying on Mr. Mysterious!

Mrs. Flores's advice:

A good detective searches for clues. You have to find something unusual or unexpected. Something ordinary that's out of place. In short: a lead.

Mr. Mysterious's parrot

The parrot! It must have come from a a pet shop. There's one at the mall. The investigation will start there.

First goal: convince my mother to take me, without revealing why.

only seen once
Where is it now?

eureka! but it's good that

THAT'S A VERY GOOD LEAD, CICI. THAT'S ALL THE ADVICE I HAVE FOR NOW...

BUT DON'T FORGET TO FILL ME IN ONCE YOU'VE SOLVED THIS EXCELLENT MYSTERY!

ABSOLUTELY, MRS. FLORES!

GOOD NIGHT, CICI.

BYE, MRS. FLORES. AND THANKS AGAIN!

I'M GOING TO HAVE TO BE SNEAKY WITH MOM...

THE NEXT DAY...

THANKS FOR TAKING ME TO THE MALL, MOM!

I'M HAPPY TO, SWEETIE!

THE GALLERY mall

Garden DIY

I THINK A HAMSTER IS A GREAT IDEA FOR ERICA'S BIRTHDAY.

MMM.

little pals

LIVE FOR LESS

OH, CICI, THEY'RE ALL SO CUTE! OOOH!

THANK YOU FOR VISITING LITTLE PALS!

WHICH DO YOU WANT?

THAT 'UN!!!

EXCUSE ME, SIR...

DID YOU SELL A PARROT TO AN OLD MAN RECENTLY?

NO, SORRY! WE DON'T SELL PARROTS.

OKAY, THANKS ANYWAY.

HEY, WAIT!

THAT'S IT!

THANK YOU FOR VISITING LITTLE PALS!

DIY City

paint

THE PAINT!

AN OLD MAN, YOU SAY? HMM...

THAT SOUNDS LIKE MICHELANGELO.

MICHELANGELO?

YEAH! THAT'S WHAT WE CALL HIM!

Michael Langer. We call him "Michelangelo." With all the paint he's bought the past 15 years, he could have painted the whole town by now! In every color!

IF YOU WANT TO WAIT, HE'LL BE BACK THIS EVENING.

'CAUSE OF THAT DOWNPOUR YESTERDAY.

THE PAINT ISN'T VERY WATERPROOF.

THANKS A LOT! YOU'RE THE BEST!

GLAD TO HELP, HON!

CICI?!

I'VE BEEN LOOKING ALL OVER FOR YOU!

SORRY. I'M READY TO GO NOW.

WHAT ABOUT THE HAMSTER?!

LENA CAN GET IT.

I'VE BEEN GOING IN CIRCLES FOR HOURS!

WHERE IS THAT WALL?!

WHA—?! OH NO!!!

MY NEW T-SHIRT!

IT'S SNAGGED!

RATS! I'VE HAD IT! I GIVE UP! I'M TIRED!

TIRED!

TIRED!

WHAT WAS THAT?!

TIRED! OSCAR'S TIRED! HE'S GOING UP TO BED!

WAIT!

HOLD ON! WAIT!

TIIIRED!

31

Behind the wall I discovered:
an abandoned zoo
some fabulous animal
paintings!
↳ Must tell Lena so
she can take photos.

I SHOULD BE TAKING NOTES...

OH, WOW!

YOU GUYS ARE FUNNY!

AHA! THERE YOU ARE! DID YOU COME TO ADMIRE YOUR PORTRAIT?

HE ISN'T AS TALKY AS YOU ARE!

TALKY!

TALKY!

CAPTAIN FLINT IS TALKY!

WOW!

HEY!

?!

OSCAR

OH...

YOU "WENT UP TO BED." BUT YOU NEVER WOKE UP, RIGHT?

Do research on the zoo. Did Oscar really exist? What happened to him?

OSCAR!

OSCAR IS TIRED!

I'M BEGGING YOU, CAPTAIN FLINT. STOP SAYING THAT OVER AND OVER!

!!!

CAPTAIN FLINT IS TALKY!

CAPTAIN FLINT ON DECK!

CAPTAIN, YOU TALK TOO MUCH.

OSCAR

QUICK! SOMEWHERE TO HIDE!

FOLLOW ME, CAPTAIN FLINT. I'VE BROUGHT SOMETHING TO FEED THE POLAR BEARS.

CAPTAIN FLINT ON DECK! AHOY, MATEYS!

THESE BUCKETS KEEP GETTING HEAVIER!

LOOK AT THEM, CAPTAIN FLINT. THEY'RE FAMISHED!

MUSTN'T KEEP 'EM WAITING...

?!! WHAT'S HE DOING???

Secret revealed:

Michael is a great animal painter!

CICI?

I THOUGHT SHE WAS WITH YOU?!

OH, HI, GIRLS!

UHHH...OH, THAT'S RIGHT! WE SHOULD GO LOOK FOR HER AT THE HIDEOUT!

WE JUST FORGOT! OKAY, UH... WE SHOULD GO!

HEH HEH...

OKAY, SOUNDS GOOD!

OH, HAPPY BIRTHDAY, ERICA!

I HOPE YOU'RE LIKING THE LITTLE HAMSTER!

?!

THE LITTLE...? UH...YES, YES! HE'S VERY CUTE!

MY BIRTHDAY ISN'T FOR FOUR MONTHS, AND I'M ALLERGIC TO HAMSTERS!

EITHER HER MOTHER'S GOING NUTS...

...OR OUR FAVORITE DETECTIVE IS HIDING SOMETHING FROM US!

THAT SOUNDS LIKE CICI!

OOOH, SHE'S GOING TO GET IT!

45

THE PARROT BROUGHT ME HERE.

GOOD OLD CAPTAIN FLINT!

HAVE YOU BEEN HERE LONG?

YEAH, KIND OF...

HMM. TELL ME... DO YOU LIKE THE PAINTINGS?

OH YES! YOU'RE VERY TALENTED!

YOUR PAINTINGS ARE ABSOLUTELY MAGNIFICENT!

THAT'S NICE OF YOU. BUT ALL I'M DOING IS CLUTCHING AT OLD MEMORIES...

WHAT IS THIS PLACE?

OH, THAT'S A LONG STORY.

THAT'S OKAY! I LOVE STORIES! I'M GOING TO BE AN AUTHOR SOMEDAY.

AN AUTHOR, EH? THEN I GUESS I MUST TELL YOU THE FULL AND PROPER TALE.

THIRTY YEARS AGO, THIS ZOO WAS ONE OF THE MOST FAMOUS IN THE COUNTRY. PEOPLE CAME FROM FAR AWAY TO VISIT. YOU COULD SEE MANY EXOTIC SPECIES, AND THE ANIMALS WERE TREATED WITH LOVE AND RESPECT. CHILDREN WERE UTTERLY ENCHANTED BY THE INCREDIBLE CREATURES HERE.

BACK THEN, I WORKED HERE AS A PAINTER, DECORATING THE HABITATS AND THE PUBLIC AREAS. THE MODELS FOR MY PAINTINGS WERE ALL AROUND ME.

BUT AS TIME WENT BY, FEWER AND FEWER VISITORS CAME. THE NEW AMUSEMENT PARKS OFFERED BIGGER AND BIGGER THRILLS. THE ZOO COULDN'T COMPETE.

WITH NO VISITORS, THE ZOO FINALLY HAD TO CLOSE ITS GATES. THE ANIMALS LEFT THEIR HABITATS TO GO LIVE IN OTHER ZOOS THAT WERE LARGER AND LESS FRIENDLY...

...AND BEFORE LONG, THE PLACE WAS ABANDONED.

I CAME BACK HERE, MANY YEARS LATER, BUT PEOPLE HAD FORGOTTEN THIS PLACE EVEN EXISTED.

STANDING AMONG ALL THE EMPTY HABITATS, I GOT THE IDEA TO BRING BACK THE ANIMALS WHO LIVED HERE, IN MY OWN WAY.

BUT I DIDN'T JUST WANT TO PAINT THEM ON A GRAY WALL.

I WANTED EACH ONE TO LIVE A LIFE, LIKE THE REAL ANIMALS DID. SO I PAINTED THE ADULTS AND THEIR LITTLE ONES. I GAVE THEM EACH A NAME. AND IN MY PAINTINGS, THEY EAT, GROW UP...

...DIE...

YOU HAVE SEEN OSCAR THE LION.

HE WAS THE KIDS' FAVORITE, THE MOST MAJESTIC OF THE BEASTS.

BUT EVENTUALLY THE YEARS CAUGHT UP WITH HIM, AND THE KIDS LOST INTEREST.

BEFORE I LEFT THE ZOO, I PAINTED HIM ONE LAST TIME...

...AND I'VE LET TIME DO THE REST.

CICI!

WE'VE BEEN WAITING AND WAITING!

WHAT DID YOU FIND THIS TIME? A HAUNTED HOUSE? AN OGRE'S CAVE?

BETTER THAN THAT!

I WENT ON THE OTHER SIDE OF THE WALL!

OH, GREAT NEWS!

LISTEN, I DON'T HAVE TIME TO EXPLAIN, BUT I'M GOING TO NEED YOU!

IT'S IMPORTANT!

WHAT A SURPRISE...

HERE WE GO AGAIN!

HERE'S WHAT WE'RE GOING TO DO...

Lena took great photos of us working in the zoo. She gave me some as souvenirs!

We all helped clean it up.
Even Captain Flint!

The broken glass was very fragile.
And very dangerous. Luckily, Michael had
lots of work gloves to lend us.

But even so, we had some casualties...
For once, Erica had a good reason to
complain!

We figured out right away that we
couldn't do it alone. So we quietly
began to get our friends to come help.

I took that one, so Lena could be in a few photos. Now you can see that she worked hard too!

We all worked really hard. But some of the big repairs were too much for us!

Lena is a great photographer. What is Michael thinking right now? Is he sad? Happy?...

One month of work, and we all kept it secret! We were so proud of ourselves! When Lena took this photo, she was so afraid to mess up the shot that she missed the timer! ☺

SEE YOU LATER, MOM!

ALEX! WAIT!!! WHERE ARE YOU...

THAT'S SO STRANGE!

HE DOES THIS EVERY WEEKEND NOW! HE ZIPS OFF, HE'S GONE ALL DAY, AND HE COMES BACK COVERED IN DIRT AND MUD!

MINE IS JUST THE SAME! AND THE LITTLE GIRL NEXT DOOR TOO.

HMM... I DON'T KNOW WHAT THEY'RE HIDING FROM US...

...BUT IT'S ALL VERY STRANGE!

I CAN'T EVEN BEGIN TO GUESS!

PSST...
CICI...

YOU'RE OFFICIALLY FORGIVEN FOR MAKING US LIE TO YOUR MOM.

THANKS! BUT I'M NOT SURE MY MOM WOULD AGREE.

LOOK! IT'S FINISHED!

TA-DA, CHILDREN! A NEW ARRIVAL IN THE ZOO!

BRAVO!

SO CUTE!

CLAP CLAP CLAP!

WOW!

SO, CHILDREN. WHAT WOULD YOU LIKE TO NAME THE CUB?

LEO!

TIGER!

OSCAR!

KIKI!

TIGGER!

ROGER!

NO, NOT OSCAR! OSCAR'S THE LION!

HEY—WHO'S THAT...?

CLAP CLAP! CLAP!

OSCAR! OSCAR'S TIRED! HE'S GOING UP TO BED!

CLAP CLAP!

CONGRATULATIONS, SIR! YOU ARE A MASTER ARTIST!

MRS. FLORES!!!

For the first time, I shared a big secret with my mom. Could she feel my hand shaking?

AND OVER THE FOLLOWING DAYS...

HELLO, GUY! I BROUGHT COFFEE!

WONDERFUL! MY CREW IS ALMOST DONE WITH THE STONEWORK. THE CEMENT IS DRYING NOW. THE BUILDING IS LIKE NEW!

COFFEE, ULYSSES?

THANKS, CICI! LOOK, I'M ALMOST FINISHED PRUNING THE HEDGES, AND I'VE REPLANTED ALL THE FLOWERBEDS!

HELLO, LOVEBIRDS! WANT SOMETHING TO DRINK?

I WANT TO FINISH UP THESE TILES FIRST!

I'D LOVE A SODA. IT'S REALLY HOT!

EVERYTHING OKAY, MOM?

YES! I'M FINALLY DONE WITH THE FLAMINGO POOL. THE SEA LIONS ARE NEXT!

WHAT ARE YOU DOING?

OH, I'M LETTING MY PEN FLOW. THIS PLACE IS VERY INSPIRING!

A NEW BOOK?

MAYBE!

Wow! I'm going to be the heroine of a book! And Mrs. Flores promised me I can help write it!

A. Flores

60

THERE ARE THE MAMMALS...

OVER THERE ARE THE REPTILES AND THE AQUARIUMS...

UH, IS SOMETHING WRONG?

AND HERE'S THE AVIARY...

NO, NO. I...WAS JUST THINKING...

WHAT IF IT ALL HAPPENS AGAIN, CICI?

WHAT IF PEOPLE GET TIRED OF MY PAINTINGS AND ABANDON THE ZOO FOR A SECOND TIME?

I DON'T THINK I COULD BEAR IT!

BUT...TODAY IS WHAT'S IMPORTANT. WE'VE GIVEN IT A SECOND LIFE! THAT'S WHAT YOU WERE ALWAYS HOPING FOR WITH YOUR PAINTINGS, RIGHT?

WELL... YOU'RE RIGHT.

I'M STEPPING OUT OF MY SECRET GARDEN, AND I GUESS I'M A LITTLE SCARED!

BE BRAVE! AFTER TOMORROW, THERE'LL BE NO GOING BACK!

The zoo has only been open a little while, but I've already collected a lot of newspaper articles!

News in Brief

Two weeks ago, a zoo in a small provincial town reopened its gates, twenty-five years after closing them. But it features a whole new kind of animal exhibit. Here, there are no animals in cages. No roars or squawks—only the sounds of visitors' footsteps and the laughter of children.

In this museum-like zoo, immense canvases await the curious. There are more and more each week: amazingly realistic animal frescoes, the work of one man, Michael Langer. The one-time official painter for this zoo, he's deeply passionate about animals. The crowds flocking to this zoo come not only for his talent but also for the style that he has developed. For Michael never stops with just one animal scene.

He constantly retouches every scene, making them evolve to suit his wishes and to reflect the passage of time.

As you can imagine, a fabulous journey awaits visitors here, caught up in these astonishingly rich works. The zoo is a veritable hymn to the beauty of nature, an ode of respect to life of all stripes.

An exhibit to see, and see again, for both young and old.

A.N.

Birth at the Zoo!

After several weeks, under the careful paintbrush of zookeeper Michael Langer, "Bonbon," an African elephant, has been born. The birth follows the disappearance of a mother bear too elderly to make it through the coming winter. Another big event: those who once roamed the zoo's paths as children no doubt remember Oscar, the majestic lion. He had vanished for twenty-five years, but today he has returned, more magnificent than ever. And the artist promises us that he has many wonderful years ahead of him!

C.V.

Bonbon

Michael Langer: Portrait of an Extraordinary Painter of Extraordinary Paintings

Michael Langer started painting at a very young age. A nature lover, he drew colorful animals with the precision of a naturalist. He soon mastered fur and plumage. With his canvases under his arm, he met the director of a rural zoo, who offered him a job: Michael would decorate the pathways of the zoo with animal frescoes. Ten years later, the zoo closed, and Michael found himself unemployed again. But his passion for painting had not disappeared, and his steps led him back to the heart of the abandoned zoo, where he made the decision to continue to keep its occupants alive with a startling idea—he would make the scenes evolve over time. We asked him how he came up with this idea. His response: "When I first began to paint, I was never satisfied with my work. I'm a perfectionist. So, naturally, I'd retouch my paintings constantly. Eventually, I gave a name to each animal and grew attached to them. Little by little, touch-up after touch-up, it amused me to change their poses, their behavior, to paint meals for them, to show them over every stage of their lives. It just happened naturally, almost in spite of myself."

An extraordinary exhibit, for fans of animals and art. J.C.

It's been a few months since the zoo reopened with an exhibit of a whole new kind. It's also become a place for artists to meet.

For thirty-five years, Michael Langer, creator of the 230 images on display, took the time to retouch each painting to "make them live." Today, he admits he no longer has the energy to keep up such a colossal job. But the reopening of the zoo has allowed him to meet many talented artists, and nine more painters are already on board to ensure the ongoing evolution of the works.

But his work hasn't inspired only artists. Annabelle Flores, a renowned author, released her nineteenth novel, *The Petrified Zoo*, on the occasion of the zoo's anniversary. In it we follow the incredible but true story of a little girl and a painter. It's bound to be a big hit.

B.C.

that's me!!!

Since the grand opening, Michael hasn't had a moment to himself. I don't know if he's even happ I hope he is, anyway...

A LITTLE LATER...

THE WORK YOU'VE DONE HERE IS ABSOLUTELY REMARKABLE!

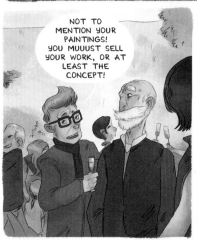

NOT TO MENTION YOUR PAINTINGS! YOU MUUUST SELL YOUR WORK, OR AT LEAST THE CONCEPT!

YOU'D BE A RICH MAN. WHAT DO YOU THINK?

MICHAEL?

UH...?

MICHAEL???

WHERE'D HE GO?

ARE YOU COMING, CAPTAIN FLINT? WE HAVE ONE LAST MISSION.

LAAAAST MISSION!

ALL HANDS ON DECK!

From Michael

From Mich

My dear Cici,

It's been so many months now since we've seen each other, and I hate that. Like me, you've been very busy, partly because of the recent events that brought us together. Because the zoo's been such a success, I'm not as free as before! But I don't regret anything. And I know that our hearts will be united forever.

Looking back, I realized that I'd forgotten something important that has to do with you. Something I'd rather tell you in person. (And I'll do so when we see each other again. I need to tell you right away, now that I've noticed I forgot!)

Thank you. Thank you for spying on me from up in your hideout, for looking for me in the woods, for having found my secret garden, and, above all, thank you for loving it, and for giving it new life.

A lot of people have been talking to me about the wealth my paintings could bring me. I could become a rich man. But the thing those people don't understand is that I'm already rich. I'm rich from all the wonderful friends I've made during the past months, rich with the laughter of kids who came to help renovate the zoo, rich with the heart of the whole town. And I owe all this wealth to you. Just as the townspeople have done for the zoo, you've made me live again.

That's my wealth. That's your gift. Thank you, Cici. For everything.

One last thing. If you have the chance, stop by and see me at the zoo. There's a new painting I'm hoping to show you. A painting that, unlike the others, will never change.

Good-bye, Cici. May you help others the way you helped me, and drive away their sadness...

With affection, Michael

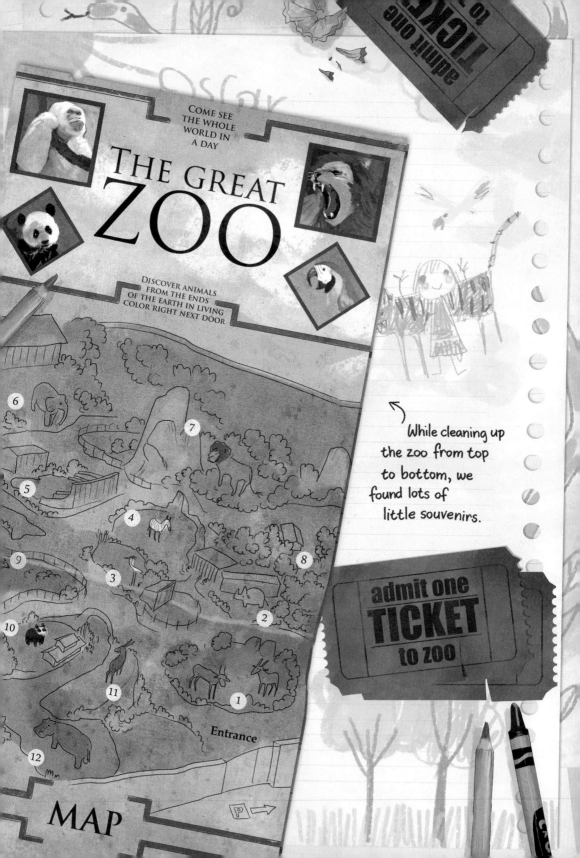

Doing research on the Internet, I came across a site called "Friends of Oscar." The story is so moving, I really wanted it to be part of my journal. I've pasted in the article.

Oscar in his enclosure at the zoo.

When he was just a cub, Oscar was the indirect victim of poachers. Facing certain death, he was saved by a veterinarian who brought him to a zoo in a small town.

Although far from his home, he nonetheless spent happy days there and had a good life. When the zoo closed, a number of people were moved to offer Oscar one last trip back to his roots. This was the birth of the "Friends of Oscar" association, which, twenty-five years later, continues to work for the well-being of animals.

Oscar passed away under the African sun on a nature reserve after a long life.

"Mr. Mysterious." That's what the girls and I called him the the first time we saw him.

From now on he's Michael the fabulous painter! I'm glad to be able to tell his story in this journal.

He was the first real mystery I solved (even though there were already some little ones before him—I'll have to write about those someday). The story of an old painter, passionate about his art, who "painted ghosts in color." Those are his words. But he did so much more than that. He gave the zoo something it was missing for a long time: a soul.

I hope I see you again soon, Michael!

And so, that's the end of this chapter. I'm very proud of it, but a little sad too. It's time to sum up the whole adventure!

My friends and I are super happy to have helped Michael. Lena took great photos, and Erica had a thousand chances to complain while we worked! I know they don't really like the way I write them into my stories, but I'm happy that it all turned out well. I'd be mad at myself if I lost my friends over that.

Mom's figured out a bit about my investigations. I think she didn't really appreciate my little fibs, but she still hasn't said anything. I'm not feeling very comfortable about it. I get the feeling she doesn't know whether to praise me for helping Michael, or to scold me for lying to her. I'd really like to go talk to her... but it's so hard!

Mrs. Flores asked me to help with writing her new book. That was so nice! She even paid me a little for it! She explained to me about "author royalties," but I didn't understand all of it.

So here it is. I've finally gone back to the zoo, like Michael asked me to. I got all teary-eyed seeing him again. And I just bawled when he showed me the famous new painting. I took a picture, and I'll keep it with me the rest of my life.

He told me: "This painting is the story of a meeting. If it had a title, this is what it would be..."

turn →

"Once upon a time..."

the end of part 1

Cici's journal

PART TWO
HECTOR'S BOOK

JORIS CHAMBLAIN
AURÉLIE NEYRET

Vacation time!!!

School will be over in two days. We put on a great show for the end of the year! I'll have lots of good memories from this school. I'm going to miss it—next year is middle school! I hope my friends and I will be in the same class. I wouldn't want to end up all alone.

Lena is an auntie! She went to her big sister's house with her parents and her little brother to help with the baby. His name is Cory and he's so cute! I can't wait to see all the pictures Lena's going to take of him.

Erica's gone off to camp for the whole month of July. A whole month to grumble about all the activities she'll be doing. Living the dream! When she gets back, she'll have a new bedroom. Her mom told me.

I'm going to be spending the whole summer at home with Mom. The mood around here isn't so great after the fibbing about the zoo. But this new journal will keep me busy while I'm waiting for the girls to get back.

July is going to be so long without them!

It's been one week since Lena and Erica left.
I hope they got my letters.

Day 9: Going to the pool with my mom this afternoon.
But does my bathing suit still fit? Swimming will do me
good...not having to think about anything...

yeeaaghh!

For the pool!

☑ bathing suit
☑ towel
☑ sunscreen
☑ goggles

☑ magazine
☑ bottle of water
☑ cookies (that won't
   end up in the bottom
   of the bag this time...)

nommm!

Day 10: The afternoon at the pool was awesome.
I crossed paths with all sorts of mysterious people. Maybe
I should start doing Mrs. Flores's writing exercises again.
But I don't know if I kept all that stuff. I'm going to look
in the attic. It's been a long time since I went up there.
I must have been 6 or 7 the last time. We had just done a
big cleanout of my room, and Mom and me carried up some
stuff to put into storage. My toys, some pictures...

When I came back down,
    I looked like this!

I found my jacket
and hat up there! They
were my great-uncle's!..

What's happened to that
other Cici I left up in
the attic, after all this
     time?

cation
venture
!!!

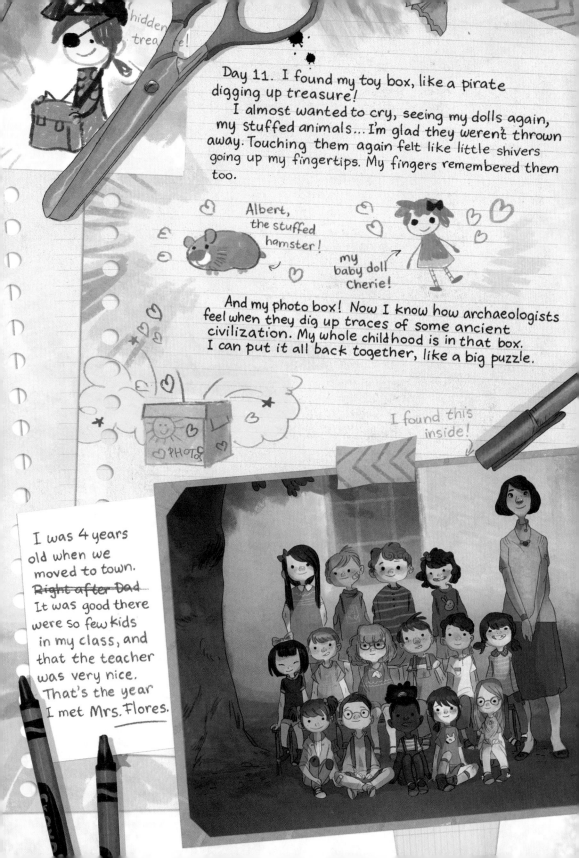

hidden treasure!

Day 11. I found my toy box, like a pirate digging up treasure!

I almost wanted to cry, seeing my dolls again, my stuffed animals... I'm glad they weren't thrown away. Touching them again felt like little shivers going up my fingertips. My fingers remembered them too.

Albert, the stuffed hamster!

my baby doll Cherie!

And my photo box! Now I know how archaeologists feel when they dig up traces of some ancient civilization. My whole childhood is in that box. I can put it all back together, like a big puzzle.

PHOTOS

I found this inside!

I was 4 years old when we moved to town. ~~Right after Dad~~ It was good there were so few kids in my class, and that the teacher was very nice. That's the year I met Mrs. Flores.

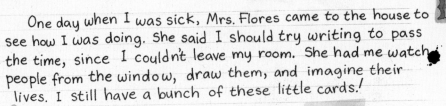

One day when I was sick, Mrs. Flores came to the house to see how I was doing. She said I should try writing to pass the time, since I couldn't leave my room. She had me watch people from the window, draw them, and imagine their lives. I still have a bunch of these little cards!

Jerome
34 years old

- Baker

- Used to be a secret agent. Good at hiding messages in the best hiding places. His job as a baker is a cover. He's spying on bad guys...

Linda
29 years old

- Head of a big charity organization

- At work all the time, she doesn't have time to take care of herself, but she takes care of others. She has a kind heart and dreams of traveling.

After I made these cards, the second part of the exercise was to make the characters meet and imagine them having an adventure. It was very funny! Then Mrs. Flores read them over and corrected the mistakes, and I copied them out neatly.

Every morning, before she goes to the office, Linda buys a pastry at the bakery. It reminds her of her childhood, when her grandmother made her breakfast.

Jerome loves when it's the right time of year to make King Cake, because he can hide a lucky charm in each cake. It's a little like his old job, except that what he's hiding this time makes people happier. This particular morning, he was all worked up, because he knew she was coming and she would choose the most golden croissant, the one with a little bit of glaze on top. He put it at the front of the case to catch her eye.

It wasn't Three Kings Day. It wasn't a cake. But in this special croissant that he made just for her, a treasure was hidden. A message. A question.

Linda left the bakery, not knowing that this croissant would change her life forever. And that forever after, it would be Jerome who made her breakfast.

Friiiiiieeeennnds!!!

dear CiCi! ☺

I hope you've found a good mystery to solve, because you sounded sort of bored in your letter. We have no free time here! It's filled with activities, biking, canoeing, lots of games. The counselors are very nice. We put on a show where we played characters from cartoons, and guess who played Grumpy? ^_^ I'm really not in a hurry to go home, it's weird there, but I wish I could see you and Lena.

Sending big kisses! Later! Erica! ♡ ☺☺

CiCi Armand
12 Des Saules
Biron 26912

Hello, Cici, how's it going? Life with Cory is nothing but diapers and breastfeeding every 2 hours, but he's sooo cute! I'm sending you a picture so you can see! Auntie Lena is completely gaga over her nephew. I remember when my little brother was a baby, even though I wasn't very old either at the time. I can't wait for you to tell me about your summer! I took lots of pictures of London, I'll show them to you! It's beautiful!

Big kisses, hon! See you soon!

Auntie Lena

★ PRINTED IN GREAT BRITAIN. LANSDOWNE PUBLISHING CO LTD. LONDON

Cici Armand
12 Des Saules
Biron 26912

★ ★ ★

On May 22nd at 4:30 pm,

Cory
made his big entrance.

He likes his parents, grandparents, young uncle, and auntie very much, so he thinks he'll stay with them a while.

Too cute, right?! Lena ☺

Hahaha super-sweetie Cory

Living for day my frie come home!

Day 16 of vacation. Mom's vacation is over, so I'm home alone. I can go out, but it's no fun without my friends. Going to the pool this afternoon, I noticed something I also saw last week. I should check it out some more. It happens every Tuesday...

Day 25 of vacation. A little note came from Mrs. Flores this morning, with a gift!!!

My dear Cici,
I hope that your vacation is going well and that you'll have plenty of things to tell me about when I get back. A change in scenery has done me a lot of good, and my new book as well. Speaking of books, I'm sending you a little something that I owe you from a while back. I hope you like the story.
Affectionately,
Annabelle

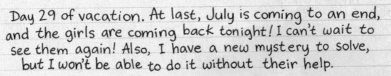

ANNABELLE FLORES
THE PETRIFIED ZOO

Wow! →
Mrs. Flores's book about Michael's story and a little bit about me!

Day 29 of vacation. At last, July is coming to an end, and the girls are coming back tonight! I can't wait to see them again! Also, I have a new mystery to solve, but I won't be able to do it without their help.

Tomorrow, we meet at the café to start the investigation!

LOOK, ERICA. SHE'S OVER THERE.

HEY, CICI!

CICI!

HUH?! SHE ASKED US HERE TO TALK ABOUT OUR VACATIONS!

RIGHT, CICI?!

WE-E-ELL ...

...ERICA'S RIGHT. I WANTED TO TELL YOU ABOUT A NEW MYSTERY...

AHA! I KNEW IT!

SO, WHAT HAVE YOU DISCOVERED THIS TIME? A PARROT THAT STUTTERS? AN UNDERGROUND FOUNTAIN OF YOUTH?

NO, NOTHING LIKE THAT. JUST SOMETHING WEIRD.

I'LL SHOW YOU.

03/07   5:20   5401

- Saw her on the 10th, around 3 pm. She left home, Mom and I went to the pool. This time I didn't pay any more attention than that.

- Saw her on the 17th, around 3 p.m. She left home, at exactly the same time as the week before. And with the same thing in her hands. I waited all afternoon to see what time she would come back. I staked out her front door from a bunch of different spots.

Her house

the café

the bench

Ulysses the florist

bus stop

- 3:05 to 4:30 p.m.: The café. I don't think I've ever drunk so many sodas!

- 4:35 to 5 p.m.: Ulysses the florist. I am SO interested in the flower display in the window—so I can peek outside! A bus passes, but she isn't on it.

- 5:05 to 5:25 p.m.: On the bench in the square watching pigeons.

- 5:30 to 5:40 p.m.: In front of the bus stop, sitting on the little wall. That thing hurts your bottom after a while. Another bus passes, but still nothing.

- 5:45 to 6 p.m.: I'm just hanging around. I really don't know what else to do. I should get a book.

- 6:05 p.m.: The bus comes, she gets out!!

Question: Does she take the bus every day, or only on Tuesday? I'll have to hang out there every day at 3 p.m. to find out.

- Wednesday: Nothing
- Thursday: Nothing
- Friday: Nothing. Imagine if Mom knew what I'm doing with my afternoons!
- Saturday: Mom and I went for a walk. I wasn't able to watch the house.
- Sunday: Mom wanted to go back to the pool. We passed the house at 3 p.m., but no sign.
- Monday: Still nothing. But I'll have a better chance tomorrow.

- Saw her on the 24th, at 3 p.m. Returned at 6:05 p.m. (This time, I had something to read.)
  Next appointment: Next Tuesday at 3 p.m.!!!

Hmph! Another case for Detective Cici

her house

the square

café

SO, CICI, WHAT'S SO SPECIAL ABOUT THIS OLD LADY?

EVERY WEEK, SHE TAKES THE BUS AT THE SAME TIME.

SHE ALWAYS SEEMS SAD WHEN SHE GOES...

AND IT'S WORSE WHEN SHE COMES BACK.

BUT THE WEIRDEST THING IS THAT BOOK. SHE NEVER PUTS IT DOWN. YOU SEE HOW SHE LOOKS AT IT?

SHE ALWAYS HAS IT WITH HER...

...LIKE IT'S HER MOST PRECIOUS POSSESSION...

COME ON...

AREN'T YOU EXAGGERATING A LITTLE?

LOTS OF PEOPLE TAKE THE BUS AT THE SAME TIME EVERY DAY! THEY GO TO WORK. TO THE GYM. THAT DOESN'T MAKE THEM "MYSTERIOUS"!

I THINK YOU'RE JUST BORED BECAUSE IT'S SUMMER VACATION.

YOU CAN THINK THAT IF YOU WANT. I DON'T CARE.

HMPH. YOU HAD US COME OVER HERE, AND NOW YOU DON'T CARE?

WHAT DID YOU NEED US FOR, ANYWAY?

90

WHAT'S THAT PAPER?

IT'S A LIBRARY CHECKOUT CARD. WITH THE SAME NAME ON IT AGAIN AND AGAIN...

...AS IF SHE CHECKS IT BACK OUT EVERY WEEK...

OH NO, I KNOW THAT LOOK, AND I DON'T LIKE IT! LEAVE IT BE. THAT POOR LADY. SHE DIDN'T DO ANYTHING TO DESERVE THIS!

I...

YOU'RE RIGHT. I SHOULDN'T POKE MY NOSE INTO SOMETHING THAT ISN'T MY BUSINESS.

WAIT, REALLY?

CICI, LETTING A MYSTERY BE A MYSTERY? PINCH ME, I'M DREAMING!

WE SHOULD PUT IT IN A MAILBOX.

93

THE NEXT MORNING...

...TO THE LIBRARY?!

YES, FOR SCHOOL. WE HAVE TO DO A REPORT ON A...UH... WAR!

WHICH ONE?

WE HAVEN'T PICKED YET!

WELL, YOU KNOW... THAT'S CICI!

OKAY, THAT'S FINE. BUT I'M SURPRISED SHE DIDN'T TELL ME ABOUT IT BEFORE.

CI—!

ALL GOOD, MOM, HERE I AM. HAVE MY CELL PHONE IN MY BAG IF I NEED IT.

WAIT, WHAT...

OF COURSE, IT HAS TO BE SET TO VIBRATE AT THE LIBRARY, SO I WON'T BE ABLE TO RESPOND RIGHT AWAY! SEE YOU THIS EVENING! KISSES!

...

ANNABELLE FLORES
THE PETRIFIED ZOO

BEST SELLER
The New Annabelle Flores

Having my own copy – that's a big deal to me. But to find it somewhere else is really something!

A SIMPLE BUT TOUCHING BOOK, BY A LOCAL AUTHOR! HAVE YOU READ IT?

MORE OR LESS...

SO, WHAT CAN I DO FOR YOU, DEAR?

YESTERDAY A LADY FROM MY NEIGHBORHOOD LOST HER CHECKOUT CARD, AND I WANTED TO RETURN IT.

OH! THANKS SO MUCH!

I'M GLAD THERE ARE STILL HONEST PEOPLE IN THIS WORLD!

IT'S BECAUSE I LOVE BOOKS. I WANT TO BE AN AUTHOR TOO, SOMEDAY!

MAYBE I'LL SEE YOUR BOOKS HERE IN A FEW YEARS. WHO KNOWS!

HA HA! I HOPE SO!

SAY, CAN I ASK YOU A QUESTION?

DO YOU KNOW WHY THERE'S ALWAYS THE SAME NAME ON THAT CHECKOUT CARD?

AHA! I RECOGNIZE THE KEEN SPIRIT OF A YOUNG NOVELIST ON THE TRAIL OF A MYSTERY!

BUT YOU'RE GOING TO BE DISAPPOINTED! SADLY IT'S NOTHING BUT A NICE OLD LADY WHO'S TAKEN OUT THE SAME BOOK FOR YEARS!

IT'S A SHAME, SINCE SHE LOVES LITERATURE! SHE USED TO WORK HERE TOO, WAY BACK WHEN.

THAT WAS BEFORE ALL THIS MESS! THIS RENOVATION NEVER ENDS...

WAIT... FOR YEARS, YOU SAY?!

I NEED TO TAKE NOTES!

THANK YOU VERY MUCH! SEE YOU SOON, AND GOOD LUCK WITH THE SHELVING!

THANKS! GOOD LUCK WITH YOUR BOOKS! HA HA!

!!!

THE PETRIFIED ZOO

OKAY, ARE YOU DONE SULKING? WHAT'S UP WITH YOU, ANYWAY?

NOTHING. CICI'S ATTITUDE BUGS ME.

I'M TIRED OF HER TELLING US WHAT TO DO ALL THE TIME!

HMPH. YOU KNOW HOW SHE IS. SHE DOESN'T DO IT TO BE MEAN. SHE DOESN'T EVEN REALIZE SHE'S DOING IT!

SPEAKING OF...

SO?

ALL DONE. I TOOK BACK THE CHECKOUT CARD. IT'S OVER.

A LITTLE LATER...

HEY, LOOK AT THIS CUTE TOP I FOUND! PRETTY, RIGHT?

MMM HMM...

I KNOW THAT FACE. SOMETHING TELLS ME YOU AREN'T REALLY DONE WITH THIS SILLY BOOK...

AM I RIGHT?

MMM HMM...

PHFFT! YOU AREN'T LISTENING AT ALL.

WE'RE INTERESTED IN YOU, CICI... YOU COULD AT LEAST PRETEND TO BE THE SAME!

YEAH, WELL, EXCUSE ME, BUT I WAS A LITTLE DISTRACTED, YOU KNOW? AND OKAY, MAYBE I ASKED FOR YOUR HELP, BUT NOBODY FORCED YOU TO COME ALONG!

DON'T WORRY. THIS IS THE LAST TIME! I'M FED UP WITH YOU USING ME!

OH, FOR... I NEVER WANT TO TALK TO YOU AGAIN!

PERFECT!

THEN I WON'T HAVE TO HEAR YOU LYING!

YOU GUYS ARE JUST KIDDING AROUND, RIGHT?

AHEM.

7:30

NO NEW MESSAGES

HELLO, YOUNG LADY.

MOM?!

I SAW LENA. SO THAT'S WHAT "RESEARCH AT THE LIBRARY" LOOKS LIKE.

WHAT?! NO!

IT'S TRUE, LENA BOUGHT SOME CLOTHES! BUT I REALLY DID GO TO THE LIBRARY!

I HAVE A HARD TIME BELIEVING THAT.

IT'S NOT LIKE YOU HAVEN'T LIED TO ME BEFORE.

!!!

105

mortar: a mortar or grenade launc[h]er is
a muzzle raised to an inclination (more [t]han
45°)

The Rose and the Mortar

I've copied down everything I found!

The cover is great.

Maybe he designed it himself?

I'd really like to know more!

Description: A young writer sent to the front lines during World War II, Hector Bertelon delivers through these letters a new look at the horror of war. A gifted writer depicts life in "The Mortar"—a secret communications battalion. Discover who these men were and plunge into the daily experience of one unit of soldiers at the heart of conflict.

Bertelon
Bertelon
Bertelon
BERTELON
? ?

Bertelon

→ I knew I'd seen his name before!

Bertelon?
Bertelon

1: works by numerical classification (old classification) "The Rose and the Mortar." Work 86-R-43.

2: works, classified by genre, (new classification) "The Rose and the Mortar," no reference...

??   ??

YESSS!!! I KNOW WHERE I'VE SEEN THAT NAME BEFORE!!!

ON MS. RONSIN'S MAILBOX!

IT'S GOT HER NAME ON IT, AND ALSO THE NAME OF...I'M GUESSING HER LATE HUSBAND, HECTOR BERTELON!

BUT WHY WOULD SHE KEEP TAKING OUT HIS BOOK? THAT'S WHAT I DON'T KNOW...JUST LIKE I STILL DON'T KNOW EVERYTHING ABOUT THE BOOK AND THAT "MORTAR" BATTALION.

BUT THERE'S A LADY WHO CAN HELP ME WITH THAT!

CICI, TURN OFF THE COMPUTER. WE'RE SITTING DOWN TO DINNER.

HOPE YOU AREN'T TOO FULL ON COOKIES...

UH...NO. NOPE...

I'M SORRY ABOUT EARLIER, MOM.

CLEAN YOUR PLATE, PLEASE.

THE NEXT DAY...

FANTASTIC!

I'VE NEVER BEEN IN THIS ROOM.

YOUR COLLECTION IS SO IMPRESSIVE!

AND EVERYTHING IS SORTED BY SUBJECT.

When I'm an author, I'll have a library like this one!

YOU DIDN'T JUST COME HERE TO COMPLIMENT MY LIBRARY, DID YOU?

NO, YOU'RE RIGHT. I'VE DISCOVERED A WEIRD BOOK, AND I NEED INFORMATION ABOUT THE SECOND WORLD WAR AND ABOUT A BATTALION CALLED "THE MORTAR."

108

"THE MORTAR"? THAT NAME DOESN'T RING A BELL. BUT I'LL LOOK...

I CAN'T PROMISE YOU ANYTHING RIGHT AWAY.

THAT'S ALL RIGHT.

BUT YOU'LL HAVE TO BE PATIENT. I'M A LITTLE BEHIND ON MY LATEST BOOK, AND MY EDITOR IS STARTING TO SCOLD ME! ONE DAY, YOU'LL KNOW ALL ABOUT THAT.

BUT WAIT... I NEED TO FIND A WAY TO READ IT...

CAN'T YOU TAKE IT OUT OF THE LIBRARY?

HEY, WAIT!

I JUST HAVE TO CALL!

EXCUSE ME, I HAVE TO MAKE A CALL...

OH, CICI! YOU'LL NEVER CHANGE!!!

HELLO?

HELLO, YES, I'M CALLING TO RESERVE A BOOK FOR NEXT WEEK...

THE ROSE AND THE MORTAR, BY HECTOR BERTELON...

MAYBE YOU SHOULD CHANGE YOUR POINT OF VIEW SOMETIMES. IT'S IMPORTANT TO STEP BACK FROM THINGS TO ANALYZE THEM.

ESPECIALLY WHEN YOU WANT TO BE AN AUTHOR.

DO YOU REALLY THINK YOU SHOULD TAKE ADVANTAGE OF OTHERS' TRUST, JUST FOR YOUR OWN ENDS?

UH...NO... I MEAN...

UM...

...I'M GONNA HAVE TO GET BACK HOME NOW. MOM'S WAITING FOR ME...

THANK YOU.

SEE YOU SOON, CICI. AND DON'T FORGET WHAT I JUST TOLD YOU.

111

Once when she was visiting, Mrs. Flores looked out this window during our writing exercise. A while later, she asked me: "If it was Cici who passed by your window, down below, what would you write about her?" I never knew what to tell her.

HELLO, WHO'S...?

...YES, IT IS. I'M HER MOTHER.

WHAT'S THAT? ARE YOU SURE...?

ALL RIGHT. I'LL GO TELL HER...

THANKS, MISS. GOOD-BYE.

CICI? THE LIBRARY JUST CALLED. THE BOOK YOU RESERVED ON WORLD WAR II WILL BE IN TOMORROW.

OH, GREAT! THANKS, MOM!

UM... YOU OKAY?

YES, BUT I'M MAD AT MYSELF FOR NOT LISTENING TO YOU THE OTHER DAY. I WAS ANGRY, AND I DIDN'T KNOW WHETHER I COULD BELIEVE YOU ANYMORE...

SORRY TO HAVE DOUBTED YOU, SWEETIE.

IT'S ALL RIGHT. IT'S MY FAULT, AFTER ALL.

YOU KNOW WHAT? TOMORROW, I'LL TAKE YOU TO GET YOUR BOOK!

FOR REAL? OH, THANK YOU, MOM!

There are mountains of books here that haven't been catalogued yet. Because of renovations, some shelves are completely empty. There are some stacks of books that almost touch the ceiling!

The shelves of children's books are incredible. All the furniture is made for little kids, and there are lots of colorful decorations inspired by the books!

This room has welcomed many authors: historians, scientists, novelists...all the books are signed. I saw several by Mrs. Flores!

There's also a secret room where a bookbinder volunteers to come in every week to repair the most damaged books. One day I'll learn how that's done.

...AND HERE ARE THE SHELVES FOR "FLORA AND FAUNA."

A LITTLE WHILE AGO WE RECEIVED AN IMPRESSIVE COLLECTION OF WORKS FROM A YOUNG BOTANIST!

SHE DID GREAT WORK ABOUT FLOWERS.

IT'S WONDERFUL!

THIS PLACE IS MAGICAL!

HA HA! I KNEW YOU'D LIKE IT! COME SEE THE PART UNDER CONSTRUCTION. IT HAS...AN UNUSUAL ATMOSPHERE!

HERE'S THE OLD "HISTORY AND GEOGRAPHY" ROOM. IT HASN'T BEEN TOUCHED IN THIRTY YEARS!

WHEN THEY STARTED CONSTRUCTION, IT WAS ALL COVERED UP TO PROTECT THE COLLECTION FROM DIRT, BUT THE RENOVATION WAS NEVER COMPLETED.

IT'S JUST AN ARCHIVE, SINCE WE DON'T USE THE SAME CLASSIFICATION SYSTEM TODAY. THE BOOKS HAVE BEEN SLEEPING ALL THIS TIME, WAITING TO SEE THE LIGHT OF DAY...

WO-O-O-OW...

115

GOOD DAY, MISS.

HELLO, MS. RONSIN! THANK YOU FOR COMING! I CALLED BECAUSE YOU LOST YOUR CHECKOUT CARD!

OH! MY GOODNESS, HOW ABSENTMINDED OF ME... WAS IT FOUND?

ABSOLUTELY! THIS YOUNG LADY BROUGHT IT BACK TO US.

HELLO, MISS! THANK YOU FOR BRINGING BACK MY CARD.

HELLO, MA'AM. I WAS GLAD TO!

I BELIEVE SHE HAS SOMETHING SHE'D LIKE TO ASK YOU: SHE'D VERY MUCH LIKE TO BORROW THE BOOK...

OH YES?

YES, I'M... DOING A REPORT ON WORLD WAR II FOR SCHOOL, AND ON THAT VERY BOOK, ACTUALLY.

I WAS THINKING IT'D BE PERFECT FOR MY ASSIGNMENT!

WHAT IS YOUR NAME?

MY NAME IS CICI, MA'AM.

ALL RIGHT, THEN, CICI. BEFORE I HAND IT OVER TO YOU, I'LL TELL YOU ITS STORY...

116

IN THE 1940S, HECTOR BERTELON WAS A YOUNG WRITER WITH BRIGHT PROMISE.

IN ADDITION TO HIS WORK AT A LOCAL PAPER, HE WROTE NOVELS. HE WAS WORKING TOWARD A GREAT CAREER...

BUT LIFE DECIDED OTHERWISE. DRAFTED INTO THE WAR, HE GAVE UP HIS PEN FOR A GUN, LEAVING BEHIND ALL THE DREAMS OF HIS YOUTH...

HE WAS SO YOUNG WHEN HE WENT TO COMBAT. HE SAW HIS COMRADES FALL ONE AFTER THE OTHER. HE SAW THE HORROR AND THE SUFFERING...

HE CAME BACK CHANGED FROM THAT WAR. THE BOY WHO LOVED LANGUAGE AND WRITING NEVER SPOKE AGAIN UNTIL THE END OF HIS DAYS, MANY YEARS LATER...

HE NEVER SPOKE AGAIN?!

NEVER AGAIN. HE WOULD MARRY, START A FAMILY, AND SHINE THROUGH HIS TALENT, BUT HE WAS ISOLATED BY HIS MUTENESS...

BUT... WHAT ABOUT THE BOOK? WHAT IS IT?

DURING THE WAR, HE KEPT UP LETTERS WITH HIS FIANCÉE. HE TOLD HER ABOUT THE DAILY REALITIES OF WAR.

THAT BOOK IS THE COLLECTION OF ALL HIS LETTERS. HIS LAST TESTIMONY.

HERE. IT'S YOURS. AT LEAST FOR A WEEK...

THANK YOU...

THESE LETTERS... THEY WERE TO YOU, WEREN'T THEY?

THEY WERE. I WAS STILL WORKING HERE WHEN HE DECIDED TO PUT TOGETHER A COLLECTION, SOME YEARS LATER.

HE CAME WITH ME IN THE MORNINGS AND HID HIMSELF AWAY HERE, IN THE HISTORY ROOM.

HE SPENT WHOLE WEEKS IN THIS ROOM. PORING OVER HIS LETTERS, CORRECTING THEM, FINISHING THEM, DATING THEM.

HE DIED SHORTLY BEFORE CONSTRUCTION STARTED ON THE BUILDING, LEAVING HIS WORK UNFINISHED.

I FINISHED IT FOR HIM.

BUT HIS LETTERS SOUND SO COLD! SO IMPERSONAL! A SIMPLE ID NUMBER AND AN ACCOUNT WITHOUT ANY HEART...

THEY DON'T SPEAK TO YOU...

SO WHY DO YOU KEEP REREADING THEM OVER AND OVER ALL THESE YEARS?

OUT OF LOVE, CICI. HIS FACE DIDN'T LIE. HE LOVED ME. BUT HE WAS NEVER ABLE TO TELL ME... READING THIS BOOK IS A LITTLE BIT LIKE HEARING THE VOICE OF MY HUSBAND WHO COULD NO LONGER SPEAK...

BUT MAYBE YOU'RE STILL A LITTLE TOO YOUNG TO UNDERSTAND... TO UNDERSTAND WHAT ONE WILL DO WHEN ONE LOVES SOMEONE WITH ALL THEIR HEART...

120

SOME DAYS LATER...

DONE!

BUT I STILL DON'T SEE WHAT'S SO SPECIAL ABOUT IT. WHY TAKE IT OUT EVERY WEEK?

THINK, CICI, THINK!

...READING THIS BOOK IS A LITTLE BIT LIKE HEARING THE VOICE OF MY HUSBAND WHO COULD NO LONGER SPEAK...

HMM... THERE MUST BE SOMETHING ELSE!

SOMETHING MORE!

BUT WHAT?!

CICI?

LENA AND ERICA ARE HERE. THEY'D LIKE TO SPEAK WITH YOU.

OH, UH... I'LL COME DOWN.

YOU WERE VERY HARD ON HER...

CAN'T YOU SEE SHE'S NOT INTERESTED IN US ANYMORE?!

IT'S NOT ABOUT US. WHEN SHE GETS ONE OF HER MYSTERIES INTO HER HEAD, SHE DOESN'T SEE ANYTHING ELSE AROUND HER, THAT'S ALL!

MEANWHILE, SHE ONLY NEEDS US TO LIE TO HER MOTHER, AND OTHERWISE SHE IGNORES US COMPLETELY!

YOU KNOW HOW SHE IS... CAN'T YOU FORGIVE HER?

NOT ANYTIME SOON... AND NOT IF SHE DOESN'T TRY TOO!

IS OUR DEAR CICI AT IT AGAIN?

A LITTLE LATER...

WE DON'T MATTER TO HER... SHE SPENDS ALL HER TIME SPYING ON PEOPLE AND MEDDLING IN THEIR LIVES INSTEAD OF PLAYING WITH US...

WE REALLY LIKE HER "DETECTIVE" SIDE! IT'S FUN! BUT SOMETIMES, IT'S TOO...

IT FEELS LIKE SHE DOESN'T CARE. THAT WE DON'T MATTER TO HER!

I'M SO SORRY, ERICA. I'LL TRY TALKING TO HER. I PROMISE BOTH OF YOU!

THANK YOU VERY MUCH...

IS YOUR BOOK GOING WELL?

BETTER THAN THAT! I FINISHED!

Even when she was little, Erica was already complaining!

Lena's first camera! She was so happy.

Lena's little brother told us: « When I grow up, I'm going to marry both of you! »

Cici

After the merry-go-round, there's nothing like a big cotton candy to put your stomach back in place!

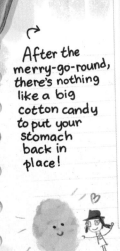

Michael...
it's been a long time since I've gone to see him at the zoo. So many memories from those days of rebuilding!

Paint fight after finishing the front gate!!!

Memories are strange. Depending on when we bring them up, or who we lived through them with, they can be sad or happy, make you smile or sigh. I love it so much that my friends were there, to laugh with me... and sometimes, I can't stand them.

IS EVERYTHING ALL RIGHT, CICI?

YES...

I SAW WHAT HAPPENED WITH LENA AND ERICA. ARE YOU GUYS FIGHTING? DO YOU...WANT TO TALK ABOUT IT?

I... I THINK IT'S MY FAULT. I...

?!

RIIIIIIING

SORRY, MOM! IT'S FOR ME!

CICI! WAIT!

CICI!!!

RIIIIIIING

HELLO?

MRS. FLORES!

I'M GLAD TO HEAR FROM YOU!

YOU FOUND SOMETHING? GREAT!

TERRIFIC!

ON THE PATIO AT THE CAFÉ, TOMORROW AFTERNOON. I'LL BE THERE!

SEE YOU TOMORROW!

THAT WAS GOOD NEWS!

AHHH! THINGS ARE ALREADY GOING A LITTLE BETTER!

THE NEXT AFTERNOON...

MRS. FLORES! HELLO!

HELLO, CICI.

SO, YOU FOUND MORE INFORMATION ABOUT THE "MORTAR" BATTALION?

NO.

NO?!

BUT...I... I DON'T UNDERSTAND...

I LIED TO YOU, CICI. JUST TO GET YOU HERE, LIKE YOU DID WITH THAT POOR WOMAN THE OTHER DAY.

BUT... WHY?

BECAUSE IT'S HIGH TIME WE SPOKE, YOUNG LADY.

YOU'VE BEEN SO INVOLVED IN YOUR MYSTERIES THAT YOU'VE NEGLECTED YOUR FRIENDS, YOU'VE LIED TO YOUR MOTHER WITHOUT THE LEAST QUALM...

AND ME... I GET THE FEELING I'M A "USEFUL" FRIEND, ONLY THERE TO PROVIDE WHAT YOU NEED. IT'S A LITTLE FLATTERING, I HAVE TO ADMIT.

BUT...BUT... NOT AT ALL. I...

LISTEN.

YOU'RE MAKING AN EFFORT. I DON'T DOUBT FOR A MOMENT THAT YOU'RE SINCERE ABOUT HOW YOU FEEL ABOUT THE PEOPLE CLOSEST TO YOU.

BUT YOU HAVE TO TRY TO OPEN UP A LITTLE MORE TO ALL THESE FOLKS AND TRUST THEM.

OR ELSE, ONE DAY, YOU'LL FIND YOURSELF ALL ALONE, AND IT WILL BE TOO LATE.

I...I'M SORRY...

I KNOW, SWEETHEART. BUT YOU SEE HOW YOU ENDED UP IGNORING YOUR FRIENDS.

AND IF I'M TELLING YOU ALL THIS, IT'S ONLY BECAUSE I KNOW YOU'RE SMART AND CAN UNDERSTAND WHAT'S AT STAKE.

YES. I UNDERSTAND.

DRY YOUR TEARS. YOU KNOW, I REALLY DID FIND SOME INFORMATION ABOUT "THE MORTAR."

IT WAS A BATTALION IN CHARGE OF SENDING CODED MESSAGES TO HEADQUARTERS.

WHAT? BUT THEN...!

SUCH A RUSH! WAIT FOR ME!

HURRY!

I'M GETTING TOO OLD FOR ALL THIS...

OH, HI, CICI! WHAT'S UP?

HI!

I ABSOLUTELY HAVE TO GET INTO THE OLD "HISTORY AND GEOGRAPHY" ROOM!

UH...WHY?

I'VE FIGURED OUT THE SECRET OF HECTOR BERTELON'S BOOK!!!

OPEN ALL THE CURTAINS?! ARE YOU SURE?

YES! IT'S BEEN WAY TOO LONG SINCE THE BOOKS GOT TO SEE SUNLIGHT!

THE BOSS IS GOING TO KILL ME...

YOU CAN SAY THAT IT'S IN HONOR OF MS. RONSIN! AND THAT'LL EVEN BE THE TRUTH!

THE LIBRARY CLOSES IN FIFTEEN MINUTES. LET'S WAIT UNTIL EVERYONE'S GONE.

A LITTLE LATER...

ALL RIGHT, MY DEAR DETECTIVE. CAN YOU REVEAL THE OUTCOME OF YOUR INVESTIGATION?

OF COURSE!

THE KEY TO THE MYSTERY IS IN HECTOR'S BOOK...

...IT HAS ALL THESE ID NUMBERS, SLIPPED IN THROUGHOUT THE LETTERS WRITTEN TO MS. RONSIN. THEY GIVE THE RANKS OF CERTAIN SOLDIERS.

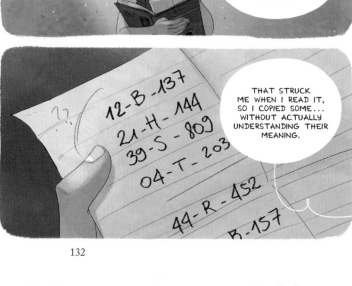

12-B-137
21-H-144
39-S-809
04-T-203
44-R-452
B-157

THAT STRUCK ME WHEN I READ IT, SO I COPIED SOME... WITHOUT ACTUALLY UNDERSTANDING THEIR MEANING.

BUT WHEN YOU TOLD ME THAT THE MORTAR, HECTOR'S BATTALION, SENT CODED MESSAGES, IT ALL BECAME CLEAR!

THOSE NUMBERS WERE REFERENCES TO SOMETHING ELSE! I REMEMBERED THAT THE LIBRARY'S OLD BOOK-SORTING SYSTEM WAS NUMERICAL...

YOU SEE THE REFERENCE NUMBERS ON THE BOOKS? THE ID NUMBERS MATCH!!!

HECTOR DIDN'T HIDE SECRET MESSAGES IN HIS LETTERS.

HE HID THEM IN THE BOOKS, THINKING THAT HIS WIFE, WHO WORKED HERE, WOULD FIND THEM!

BUT THE RENOVATIONS STALLED, AND...

LOOK!!!

WO-O-OW...

IT'S A LOVE LETTER! IT'S ADDRESSED TO "MY DEAR, SWEET AS A ROSE..."

AND THAT LETTER'S BEEN HERE ALL THESE YEARS? IT'S SO SAD...BUT SO ROMANTIC!

LET'S PUT IT BACK IN THE BOOK. IT ISN'T MEANT FOR US.

THAT'S TRUE...BUT THE PERSON THEY'RE ADDRESSED TO NEVER FOUND THEM. WE HAVE TO FIX THIS!

HERE'S WHAT WE'RE GOING TO DO...

HELLO, MS. RONSIN? IT'S THE LIBRARY...

NO, NO, YOU HAVEN'T LOST YOUR CHECKOUT CARD AGAIN, HEH! NOT THIS TIME!

I'M CALLING A BIT LATE, BUT IT'S TO LET YOU KNOW THAT YOUNG CICI'S BROUGHT BACK YOUR BOOK. SO YOU CAN COME PICK IT UP AS SOON AS YOU'D LIKE.

SURE THING! TOMORROW, THEN...

IT'S UP TO YOU NOW, CICI...

135

A LITTLE LATER...

6:43

Mom

hey mom, I'll be back in 20 minutes. Mrs. Flores is with me, later!
6:42

OK.
6:43

THERE. I'VE FINISHED THE LETTER FOR MS. RONSIN! EVERYTHING'S READY FOR TOMORROW...

...I HOPE YOU'LL BE HAPPY NOW.

I'M VERY PROUD OF YOU, CICI...

THANK YOU...

COME ALONG, NOW. I'LL SEE YOU HOME.

Dear Ms. Ronsin,

Since I'm a very curious person, I wanted to know why you were always taking out the same book. I observed you for a few weeks, and I really wanted to find out your secret.

To do that, I put my mother's trust and the friendship of my three very best friends at risk. I'm giving your book back to you, but first, I need to tell you that I made a discovery. Some people have trouble saying what's in their hearts— I know a thing or two about that. But Hector found a way to break through his silence.

I wrote the ID numbers from the letters out on a sheet of paper. I didn't really understand what they were doing in there. Those numbers intrigued me. A friend's research turned up the fact that The Mortar was a secret battalion in charge of coded messages during World War II. So I realized that the book was a code! You remember how the classification system in the library was changed after the renovation? The numbers in your husband's letters weren't ID numbers, they were really references to books where he had hidden letters for you...

One secret letter for every number.

Cici

THE NEXT MORNING...

GOOD MORNING, MISS...

GOOD MORNING, MS. RONSIN! YOUR BOOK IS WAITING FOR YOU.

BUT WE HAVE A LITTLE SURPRISE FOR YOU. WOULD YOU PLEASE COME WITH ME?

?

OF COURSE!

IT'S FOR YOU, IN MEMORY OF YOUR PAST. I'LL LET YOU... REDISCOVER THE PLACE...

UM... THANK YOU?

I...

OH!

HECTOR'S DESK...

CICI...?

WHY ARE YOU CRYING?!

IT'S NOTHING, MOM. DON'T WORRY.

I'M FEELING EMOTIONAL, THAT'S ALL!

Like I did with my first journal, where I solved the Michael mystery, I've tagged on an extra page. I wanted to go over Ms. Ronsin's life.

I went to her place to find out more. (Mom was surprised that I didn't want to go to the pool that day...)

- Elisabeth Ronsin worked at the library for 30 years, running programs to bring culture to the poorest families, to help kids in school, to create reading groups in hospitals, retirement homes, prisons...

- Her whole life was dedicated to helping others. I admire her for her courage and generosity. She's had a great career!

- She retired a few years after they started renovations on the library. She became an advisor for the new layout. The current librarian must not have known, but it was Ms. Ronsin who created the children's space and the meet-the-author forum!

- To thank me for what I did, she gave me this photo of her and Hector when they were young.

Before I left, Ms. Ronsin talked to me about the letter I wrote to her. She was overwhelmed by what I'd done to figure it all out, and she asked me to tell her about it. I gave her the embarrassing list:

- I was banished for life by the only two friends I've ever had. And it was all my fault, because I was so obsessed with the book and what it was hiding. I was so caught up in other people's lives, I ruined part of my own.

- I made the same mistake with Mrs. Flores, another friend who's very dear to me, by only using her to get stuff I wanted to know. I'm lucky she's smarter than I am and that she took the time to give me a little lesson and help me figure out some solutions. She didn't have to do that.

- With Mom, it's a little confusing. The truth became a lie, then the lie became true again. I think that something changed for the better anyway. But it's still hard to go to her and tell her all of this.

What a list!

Then Ms. Ronsin told me: "Don't make the same mistake Hector did, because when we keep what we're feeling locked inside, in the end we become the prisoner. Speak up. Don't be embarrassed by what you feel. Express your doubts, your fears. Tell the people you love that you have them in your heart. They'll always be grateful."

I'll see what I can do. I hope it's not already too late.

THE NEXT TUESDAY...

ARE... ARE YOU SURE?

COMPLETELY SURE! I'VE WANTED TO READ THESE BOOKS FOR A WHILE.

TODAY I FINALLY DECIDED TO CHECK THEM OUT!

WHAT ABOUT THE ROSE AND THE MORTAR?

AS I BELIEVE YOU KNOW, YOUNG LADY, MY TORMENT IS OVER. A GUARDIAN ANGEL RESCUED ME...

FROM NOW ON, I'M FREE!

UNTIL NEXT TUESDAY, MISS!

GOOD-BYE, MS. RONSIN!

THAT SWEET CICI...

ANNABELLE FLORES
THE PETRIFIED ZOO

REST

☒ Mrs. Flores ♡

☐ Erica and Lena ♡

☐ Mom

♡

145

THAT NIGHT...

CICI?

ARE YOU THERE?

IN THE KITCHEN, MOM!

WHY ARE THE LIGHTS... WOW!!!

SURPRIIIISE!!!

THAT WAS DELICIOUS, SWEETIE! BRAVO!

I WORKED ON IT ALL AFTERNOON, JUST FOR YOU, MOM!

YAAAAWWWN! I'M FALLING DOWN TIRED...

YOU GO TO BED, BABY. I'LL CLEAN UP.

GOOD NIGHT, MOM.

GOOD NIGHT, SWEETIE!

Ta-da! The new journal's filled up, and school is starting again. But this vacation will be carved into my memory forever.

Ms. Ronsin is volunteering a few days a week at the library. She does story time for the toddlers. I think she's gotten a taste for it again, and I'm really happy for her. I'm definitely going to help at some of her readings.

Lena picked out a million photos that she took of her nephew. Poor thing, he can still only see shapes and colors, but he's had lots of flashes in his eyes! But she hasn't forgotten her little brother, who wants her attention even more than before. He's not the littlest one in the family anymore!

It turns out that everything's mixed up at Erica's house. Two of her brothers are moving out. They're grown-up, going to school, and getting jobs. They're reorganizing the house, and everything is different for her family. It's been making Erica extra cranky, but I think it's hardest on her mom. Erica and Lena and I will pitch in to make sure there's lots of noise in the house!

Good-bye, brothers!

Hello, new bedroom!

I went to see Mrs. Flores, to read her new book and to show her the character cards I found. That brought back memories. She was happy to hear I hadn't forgotten that game, but she was surprised that two of the character cards were still blank. So they're glued in at the end of my journal, to say: "I think it's time for these two characters to meet. I'm sure they'll have a lot of things to talk about..."

I'll have to write this story now.

It's not easy to write a letter to your best friends...
I'd love a little help!

First Second

English translation by Carol Klio Burrell
English translation © 2017 by Roaring Brook Press,
a division of Holtzbrinck Publishing Holdings Limited Partnership

Published by First Second
First Second is an imprint of Roaring Brook Press,
a division of Holtzbrinck Publishing Holdings Limited Partnership
175 Fifth Avenue, New York, NY 10010
All rights reserved

Library of Congress Control Number: 2016961592

ISBN: 978-1-62672-248-4

Our books may be purchased in bulk for promotional, educational, or business use.
Please contact your local bookseller or the Macmillan Corporate and Premium Sales Department
at (800) 221-7945 ext. 5442 or by e-mail at MacmillanSpecialMarkets@macmillan.com.

FIRST

EDITION

Originally published in French in 2012 by Éditions Soleil as *Les Carnets de Cerise, Tome 1: Le Zoo Pétrifiée*
and in 2013 as *Carnets de Cerise, Tome 2: Le Livre d'Hector*
French edition © 2012, 2013 by Éditions Soleils/ Chamblain/ Neyret
First American edition 2017
Hand lettering by Carol Klio Burrell
Book design by Chris Dickey and Danielle Ceccolini
Printed in China by RR Donnelley Asia Printing Solutions Ltd., Dongguan City, Guangdong Province

10 9 8 7 6 5 4 3 2 1

BY ART
WE LIVE